MIGHTY MILITARY MACHINES

AIR FORCE ONE

BY RYAN NAGELHOUT

Gareth Stevens PUBLISHING

HOT TOPICS

Please visit our website, www.garethstevens.com. For a free color catalog of all our high-quality books, call toll free 1-800-542-2595 or fax 1-877-542-2596.

Nagelhout, Ryan.
Air Force One / Ryan Nagelhout.
pages cm. — (Mighty military machines)
Includes index.
ISBN 978-1-4824-2110-1 (pbk.)
ISBN 978-1-4824-2109-5 (6 pack)
ISBN 978-1-4824-2111-8 (library binding)
1. Air Force One (Presidential aircraft)—Juvenile literature. 2. Presidents—Transportation—United States—Juvenile literature. I. Title.

TL723.N34 2015
623.74'65—dc23

2014026082

First Edition

Published in 2015 by
Gareth Stevens Publishing
111 East 14th Street, Suite 349
New York, NY 10003

Designer: Nicholas Domiano
Editor: Ryan Nagelhout

Photo credits: Cover background, p. 1 Ensuper/Shutterstock.com; series logo Makhnach_S/Shutterstock.com; cover, pp. 1, 12 Raymond Boyd/Michael Ochs Archives/Getty Images; pp. 5, 23 Erik Simonsen/Photographer's Choice/Getty Images; p. 7 APimages.com/Charles Tasnadi; p. 8 US Air Force photo; p. 9 APimages.com; p. 11 Pool/Getty Images News/Getty Images; p. 13 Charles Ommanney/Getty Images News/Getty Images; p. 15 New York Daily News/Getty Images; p. 16 APimages.com/Kevork Djansezian; pp. 17, 21 JEWEL SAMAD/AFP/Getty Images; p. 19 PAUL J. RICHARDS/AFP/Getty Images; pp. 24, 25 MANDEL NGAN/AFP/Getty Images; p. 26 US Air Force Photo/Staff Sgt. Jerry Fleshman; p. 27 USAF/Getty Images Sport/Getty Images; p. 29 Cecil Stoughton/The LIFE Images Collection/Getty Images; p. 30 Aurin/Shutterstock.com.

Printed in the United States of America

CPSIA compliance information: Batch # CW15GS: For further information contact Gareth Stevens, New York, New York at 1-800-542-2595.

CONTENTS

READY FOR TAKEOFF

The president of the United States needs to fly somewhere. He leaves the White House and goes to an airport, just like us. But unlike us, he has his own plane waiting for him. That's Air Force One!

INTEL REPORT

Usually, any air force plane the president is flying on becomes Air Force One.

Air Force One is part of the United States Air Force, the branch of the military that operates with planes and helicopters. As commander in chief, the president leads the US military, including the air force. Air Force One helps the president fly all around the world!

INTEL REPORT

The US military started a separate air **corps** in 1920, which later became the air force.

THE "SACRED COW"

The first active president to fly in an airplane was Franklin D. Roosevelt in 1933. Called the "**Sacred** Cow," it was a Douglas C-54 Skymaster that had a sleeping area, radio telephone, and elevator for the president's wheelchair.

INTEL REPORT

Theodore Roosevelt was the first president to fly in 1910, but it happened after he was no longer president.

Presidents traveled using a number of airplanes in the 1940s and 1950s. In 1958, President Dwight D. Eisenhower added three Boeing 707 jets to the presidential **fleet**. In the early 1960s, these became known as Air Force One.

INTEL REPORT

The first airplane to use the call sign "Air Force One" was a Boeing 707 known as SAM (Special Air Missions) 970.

Today, the president has two Boeing 747-200B jets that serve as Air Force One. On the outside, each jet is white with a blue nose and says "United States of America" on the side. It also has the presidential seal and an American flag.

INTEL REPORT

The same two Boeing jets are used by the vice president but are called Air Force Two when he is flying.

CUSTOM JET

Air Force One is highly **customized** just for the president. Not many people get a chance to look inside Air Force One, but it has three separate decks like all 747s. The plane's cabin is **divided** into many separate rooms.

INTEL REPORT

There are three different doors you can use to enter Air Force One.

Air Force One doesn't look much like a plane on the inside. Its many rooms are rectangles with different chairs and tables in them. Some rooms look like offices, while others look like **conference** rooms.

INTEL REPORT

Air Force One has its own Oval Office on the right side of the plane near the cockpit.

THE SUITE

The president has his own suite, or a set of rooms, on Air Force One. The suite is below the cockpit and includes a dressing room, shower, and a gym. Air Force One also has a doctor's office and a dining room.

INTEL REPORT

Air Force One's kitchen can feed 100 people at a time and has 2,000 meals on hand at all times.

Air Force One flies more than just the president from place to place. Lots of officials and the president's staff fly in Air Force One. Reporters who cover the president fly on Air Force One, too. They have to pay for their trip, though!

INTEL REPORT

Reporters flying on Air Force One even get to pick their own in-flight movie!

SAFETY FIRST

Air Force One is very safe. It's made of special strong glass and metal in case of an attack. It also has things like flares to confuse missiles. It can even refuel in the air in case it can't land.

INTEL REPORT

Air Force One can act like a **mobile** White House if there are problems on the ground.

FLYING TO ANDREWS

Air Force One is stationed at Andrews Air Force Base in Maryland. When the president needs to use Air Force One, a US Marines helicopter lands at the White House and is used to take the president to Andrews Air Force base for takeoff.

INTEL REPORT

Marine One is the name of any U.S. Marine aircraft carrying the president.

Before Air Force One takes off, other air force planes land where it's heading. The planes, C141 Starlifters, carry with them the president's **motorcade**. These limos, vans, and other **equipment** help keep the president safe on the ground.

INTEL REPORT

Air Force One's flight crew and staff are all members of the air force.

TAKING FLIGHT

Once the president is on board Air Force One, it's time for takeoff. The jet roars down the Andrews Air Force Base runway and lifts off the ground. The president is off to travel the world on one of the coolest airplanes in the world!

INTEL REPORT

In November 1963, Lyndon Johnson became president on board Air Force One when President Kennedy was killed in Dallas, Texas.

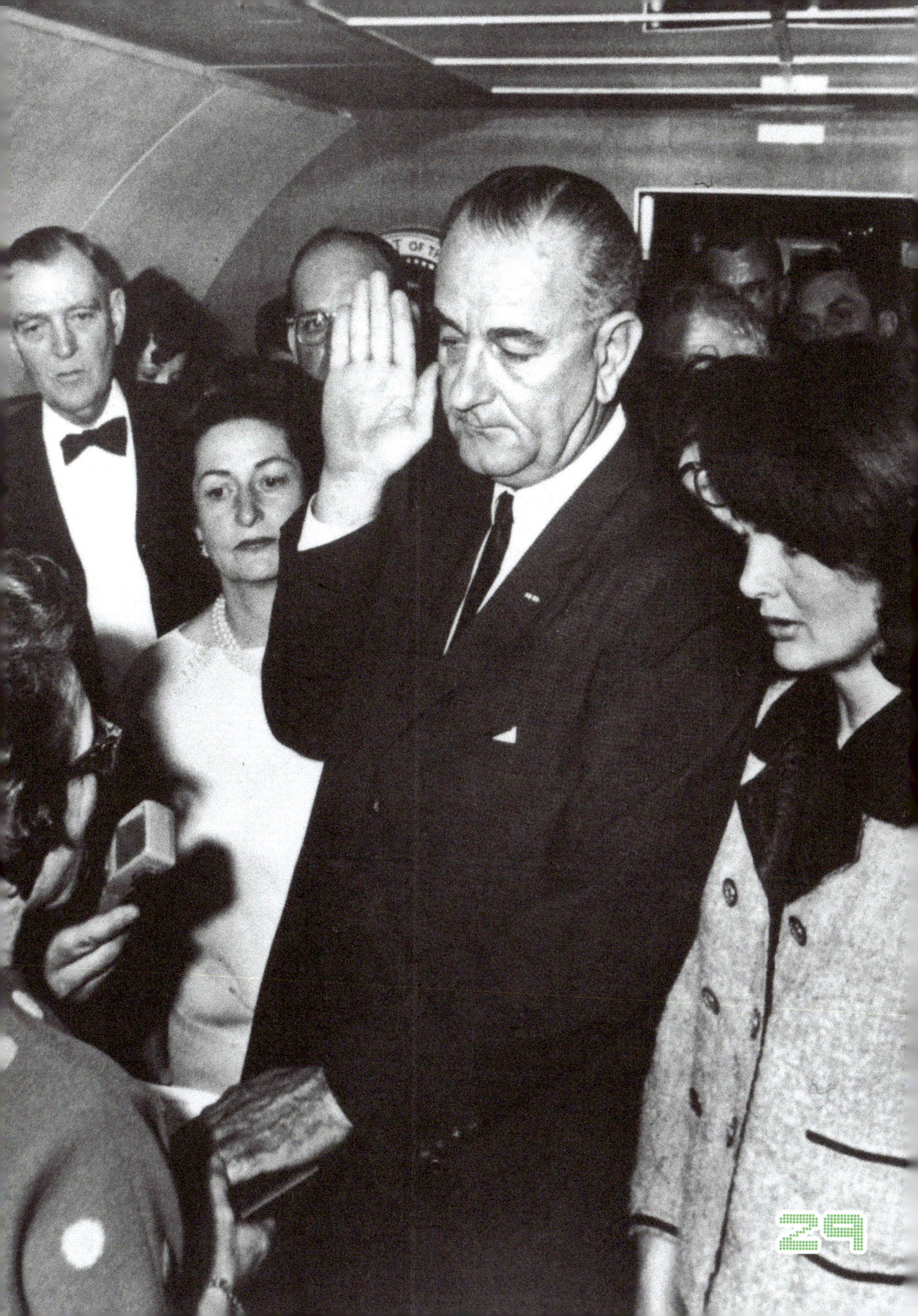

INSIDE AIR FORCE ONE

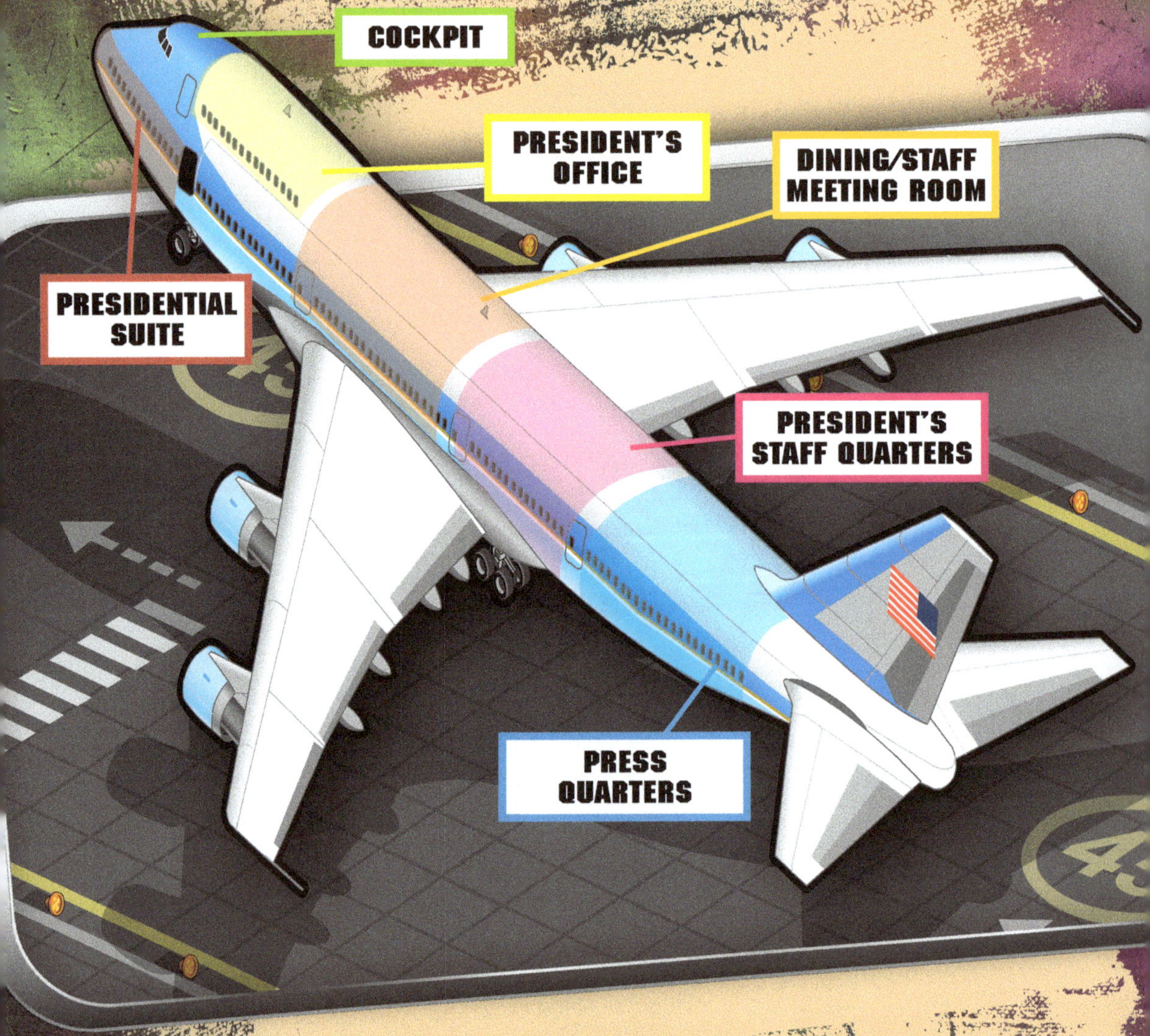

FOR MORE INFORMATION

Books

Mattern, Joanne. *Air Force One*. New York, NY: Children's Press, 2014.

Miller, Amanda. *What Is Air Force One?* New York, NY: Children's Press, 2009.

Websites

Air Force One
whitehouse.gov/about/air-force-one
Read more about Air Force One's history on the official White House site.

Air Force One
whitehousemuseum.org/special/AF1/
Find out more about Air Force One's history.

How Air Force One Works
people.howstuffworks.com/air-force-one.htm
Learn more about what's inside Air Force One.

Publisher's note to educators and parents: Our editors have carefully reviewed these websites to ensure that they are suitable for students. Many websites change frequently, however, and we cannot guarantee that a site's future contents will continue to meet our high standards of quality and educational value. Be advised that students should be closely supervised whenever they access the Internet.

GLOSSARY

conference: a meeting

corps: an organized branch of the military

customized: built for a specific person

divide: to separate

equipment: tools, clothing, and other items needed for a job

fleet: a group of planes under one command

mobile: able to move

motorcade: a parade of cars

sacred: holy or deserving honor

INDEX